THE GUNPOWDER PLOT

Wri... ...an

ABOUT THE PLAY

The Gunpowder Plot can be used during Shared or Guided Reading sessions, with individuals or small groups of children, or performed by all the class with individual children taking on the roles of the named parts and the rest of the class playing the parts of extras, such as the soldiers, guards, Lords and Ladies and ordinary Londoners.

This play is based on the true event of the Gunpowder Plot, however the characters and story are fictitious. The play can be used when learning about the Plot and to explore what life was like under the Stuarts in 1605.

Sets and props

Making the sets and props for the play will be more than half the fun. You'll need to do some research first – what did London and houses look like in the seventeenth century? Once you know what you want to show in your scenes, you could tape together some white paper to make some large backdrops for the play that can be painted to create the sets; you will need a backdrop for the streets of London, the Palace of Whitehall, a London tavern, the plotters's house, outside the Houses of Parliament and, of course, the cellars.

You can perform the play without having to find lots of different props. All you need are some barrels of gunpowder and some lanterns, which you can make from cardboard. You can use some sheets of A4 paper from your classroom for the plotters's documents in scene three.

Staging

There is no need to put on a huge production. All you need is a space where you can put on the play. With a small group you could use part of the classroom – perhaps the area where you usually read your stories. Or you could move the furniture back and use the whole room. If the whole class is involved, a hall or even the school field will give you all the space you need.

Costumes

Costumes can also be kept simple and you can be very creative with ideas of costumes for each character. What did men, women and children wear in 1605? Remember that the rich and poor dressed in very different clothes. The rich wore lots of big frilly shirts and huge dresses. Very strange wigs were also fashionable and you could make your own from string and cotton wool. The poor plotters could be in a shirt and brown trousers to show they are different from the king and the richest people.

HAVE FUN PUTTING ON YOUR PLAY!

Go to www.waylandbooks.co.uk for more ideas.

Introduction

It is 1605 and the Protestant King James I has been on the throne for two years. Several attempts have already been made on his life by England's Catholics. In a few weeks it will be the 5th November – the State Opening of Parliament. The king and all his supporters will be there. The perfect opportunity for anyone who wants to kill them all…

The characters in the play

 Narrator

 King James I

 Sir Robert Cecil

 Jack Lambert

 Baron Monteagle

 The Duke of Suffolk

 Robert Catesby

 Thomas Wintour

 John Wright

 Thomas Percy

 Robert Keyes

 Guy Fawkes

 Mrs Ashby

 Palace Guards

 Soldiers

Extras: Londoners and Courtiers

SCENE 1

CHARACTERS IN THIS SCENE:

● **Narrator** ● **King James I** ● **Cecil** ● **Jack**

The year is 1605 and **King James I** *is sitting in his study at the Palace of Whitehall.*

● **Narrator:** King James I is frowning as he reads some papers at his desk in the Palace of Whitehall.

Somebody knocks on the door.

● **King James:** *(calling)* Come in!

Cecil *and his assistant,* **Jack** *enter.*

● **Narrator:** Sir Robert Cecil and his young secretary Jack Lambert enter.

● **Cecil:** Good morning, Your Majesty. *(bowing)* I see you're reading my report.

● **King James:** I wish I wasn't, Cecil. I didn't realise quite so many people hated me!

Cecil: Oh, I don't know about that, Your Majesty.

King James: But this is a list of plots against me!

Cecil: We have the latest figures. Tell the king, Jack.

Jack: *(flustered, leafing through the papers he's holding)* There were two main plots, Your Majesty, but about another ten or so minor ones.

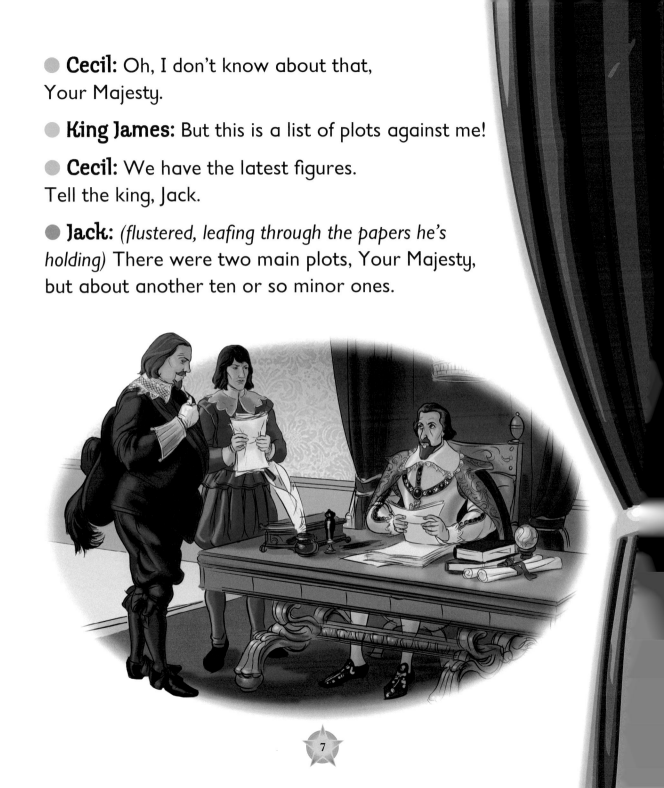

● **Cecil:** But don't worry, Your Majesty. Everything is under control.

● **King James:** Really? It doesn't sound like it to me.

● **Cecil:** We've caught all the plotters, Your Majesty.

King James: *(looking surprised, but pleased)* All of them? Good work, Cecil. I can't tell you how glad I am that you're the country's top spy!

Jack: *(whispering to **Cecil**)* But Sir, what about...

Cecil: *(whispering back)* Not now, Jack. *(turning to the **king**)* Your Majesty is too kind. That's why so many people love you.

King James: I'll be happy so long as they don't try to kill me. Is everything ready for the Opening of Parliament?

Cecil: Not quite, Your Majesty. We still have a few security checks to make.

King James: Well, don't let me keep you from your work.

Cecil: *(bowing)* Your Majesty. Come along, Jack.

Jack and **Cecil** *leave, whispering to one another as they go.*

Jack: But Sir, shouldn't you have told the king about...

Cecil: ...The other plot? No, we need to find out a little more first, such as who the plotters are!

Cecil *hurries on with* **Jack** *scampering along behind him.*

SCENE 2

CHARACTERS IN THIS SCENE:

- Narrator ● Catesby ● Wintour ● Percy
- Fawkes ● Wright ● Keyes

This scene takes place in a crowded London tavern. All of the plotters have met to discuss the plot.

● **Narrator:** A few streets away from the Palace, in a dark, dingy tavern, four men are seated at a table, plotting...

● **Catesby:** So it's agreed, then. The king must die.

● **Wintour:** And all his men with him.

● **Wright:** We'll need someone to do the job.

● **Percy:** Actually, I know just the man.

● **Catesby:** Who is he?

● **Percy:** His name is Guy Fawkes. I've asked him to meet us here. *(Looks over to the bar.)* In fact, there he is!

Percy *waves at two men standing by the bar.* **Guy Fawkes** *and* **Robert Keyes** *walk to the table.*

● **Wintour:** So, Mr Fawkes. Tell us about yourself and your companion.

● **Fawkes:** *(shrugging)* There's not much to tell. Keyes and I are soldiers and we've been fighting for the Spanish king, killing Protestants in Holland.

● **Keyes:** Oh yes, Sir, we hate Protestants!

● **Wright:** Er... quite. *(smiling)* Well, you're with friends here.

● **Fawkes:** *(nodding)* I'm glad to hear it. There aren't many people in England I'd call friends these days. So why did you want to meet us?

● **Catesby:** Tell me, Fawkes, have you done any work with gunpowder before?

● **Fawkes:** *(shrugging again)* We've blown up loads of stuff, haven't we, Keyes?

● **Keyes:** Oh yes, Sir. We like to make things go with a bang!

● **Percy:** *(grinning)* I told you Fawkes would be perfect!

● **Catesby:** Good, come with me, Fawkes. I've got something to show you.

SCENE 3

CHARACTERS IN THIS SCENE:

● **Narrator** ● **Catesby** ● **Mrs Ashby** ● **Percy**
● **Fawkes** ● **Wright** ● **Keyes** ● **Wintour**

*The plotters are in a small room in a house they have rented from the landlady, **Mrs Ashby**.*

● **Narrator:** A few weeks later, in a small house near the Palace of Westminster – the great building where Parliament meets – the plotters are arguing!

● **Fawkes:** *(angrily banging on the table)* I've never heard of anything so stupid!

● **Percy:** Calm down, Fawkes, and let Catesby explain the plan again.

● **Catesby:** I rented this house because it's next door to the Palace of Westminster. We just need to dig a tunnel...

● **Percy:** ...put in the barrels of gunpowder and boom!

● **Keyes:** I'm not doing any digging!

Fawkes: It just won't work, anyway. It would take weeks!

Wintour: Plus, I don't want any innocent people killed.

Wright: I agree. I think we've got far too much gunpowder.

There's a knock at the door and everybody freezes.

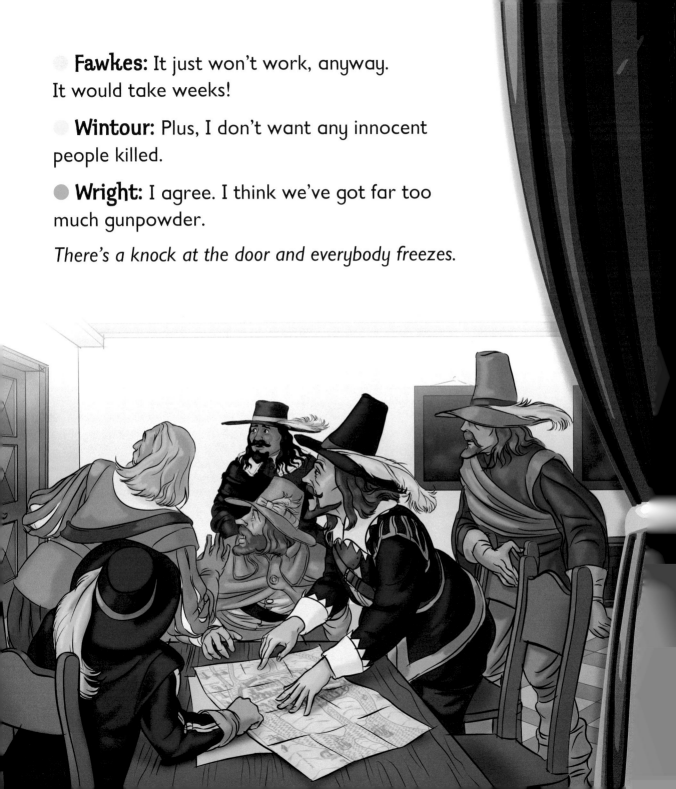

● **Catesby:** *(nervously calls out)* Who's there?

● **Mrs Ashby:** It's Mrs Ashby, your landlady!
I just wanted to make sure everything was all right.

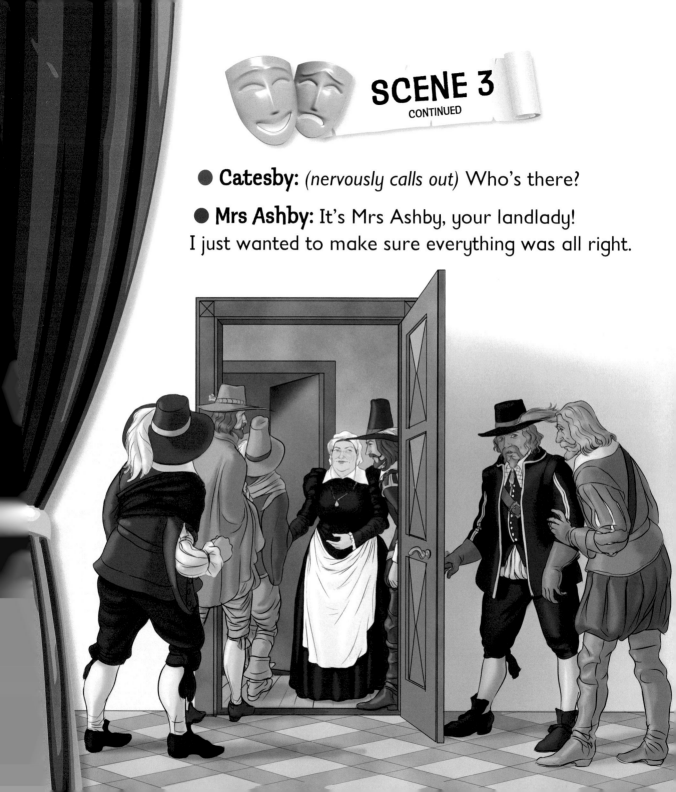

● **Catesby:** *(sighing)* Everything is fine, Mrs Ashby.

● **Mrs Ashby:** Good. I also realised that I hadn't told you about the cellar.

● **Catesby:** *(looking up from the plans sharply)* Cellar? What cellar?

Mrs Ashby *opens the door and enters the room.*

● **Mrs Ashby:** *(talking as she enters)* The one under the house, of course! You can store things in it if you like, no extra charge. It's really big.

● **Catesby:** *(looking interested)* Is that so?

● **Mrs Ashby:** Oh yes, it even connects to the cellar under the Palace next door. Would you like to see it?

● **Catesby:** Oh, most definitely, Mrs Ashby... lead on!

Catesby, **Percy**, **Fawkes** *and* **Keyes** *follow* **Mrs Ashby** *out.*

● **Wintour:** *(holding* **Wright** *back)* I can't let any innocent people die, Wright.

● **Wright:** Neither can I. I think we ought to write a letter...

Wintour *and* **Wright** *whisper as they hurry after the others.*

SCENE 4

CHARACTERS IN THIS SCENE:

- Narrator
- Cecil
- Suffolk
- Monteagle
- Jack
- Palace Guards
- Extras – Lords and Ladies

*Cecil and Jack are outside the Houses of Parliament, taking charge of a lot of **guards**. Many **Lords** and **Ladies** are arriving to greet the **king**, among them two of **Cecil**'s friends, **Monteagle** and **Suffolk**.*

● **Narrator:** It's the morning of the Opening of Parliament. Cecil and Jack are at the main entrance giving orders to the Palace Guards...

● **Cecil:** *(talking to the **guards**)* Stay sharp, men. I need you to be alert today!

*Enter **Monteagle** and **Suffolk**.*

● **Suffolk:** Ah, there you are, Cecil. Monteagle and I have been looking for you.

● **Cecil:** Well, you've found me. What's that you've got there, Monteagle?

● **Monteagle:** *(handing **Cecil** a letter)* We weren't quite sure, old boy. But we thought you ought to take a look at it.

Cecil: *(reading the letter)* 'Everyone who loves not the king should stay away from the Palace of Westminster and our hell-fire on November 5th...' *(looking at* **Monteagle***)* Why, that's today! Where did you get this?

Monteagle: Someone put it through my door last night. Could be a prank, mind you.

Suffolk: It's all very strange. What in heaven's name is 'hell-fire'?

Jack: Sir, do you think it might mean... *(gulping)* gunpowder?

Cecil: I'm sure of it! This must be from one of the plotters. Someone who doesn't want to kill too many people...

Monteagle: I say, what a clever fellow you are, Cecil!

Cecil: We need to search the building. Jack, round up more guards.

Jack: Right away, Sir.

Cecil: Monteagle, Suffolk, take some men and search the cellars. There's not a moment to lose!

Everyone runs off in different directions.

SCENE 5

CHARACTERS IN THIS SCENE:

- Narrator
- Suffolk
- Monteagle
- Fawkes
- Keyes
- Cecil
- Soldiers

Suffolk, **Monteagle** *and three* **soldiers** *are in the cellars below the Palace of Westminster.*

● **Narrator:** A little while later, Suffolk and Monteagle are searching the cellars under the Palace with a few soldiers.

● **Monteagle:** Remind me why we're down here again?

● **Suffolk:** I don't have the foggiest idea.

● **Monteagle:** Wait! *(pause)* Did you hear something?

Fawkes *and* **Keyes** *suddenly appear from around a corner.*

● **Soldier:** Halt! Who are you?

● **Fawkes:** I'm, er… John, er, Johnson…

● **Monteagle:** John Johnson? What a curious name!

Suffolk: Have either of you men seen anything or anyone suspicious?

Fawkes: No, Sir, we've just been stacking wood, eh, Keyes?

Keyes: That's right, Guy... I mean John.

Monteagle: *(nodding)* Very good. Let us know if you see anything.

Fawkes: Of course, Sir. You can trust us.

Fawkes and **Keyes** *walk off, sniggering while* **Monteagle** *and* **Suffolk** *keep looking. Soon* **Cecil** *comes to find them.*

Cecil: Well, the king has just arrived. Did you find anything?

Monteagle: Not really, we did meet some nice chaps, though. *(Pauses and suddenly looks aghast.)* Come to think of it, perhaps they shouldn't have been down here...

Cecil: What! Jack, guards, follow me!

SCENE 6

CHARACTERS IN THIS SCENE:

- Narrator
- Suffolk
- Fawkes
- Keyes
- Cecil
- King James
- Jack
- Palace Guards

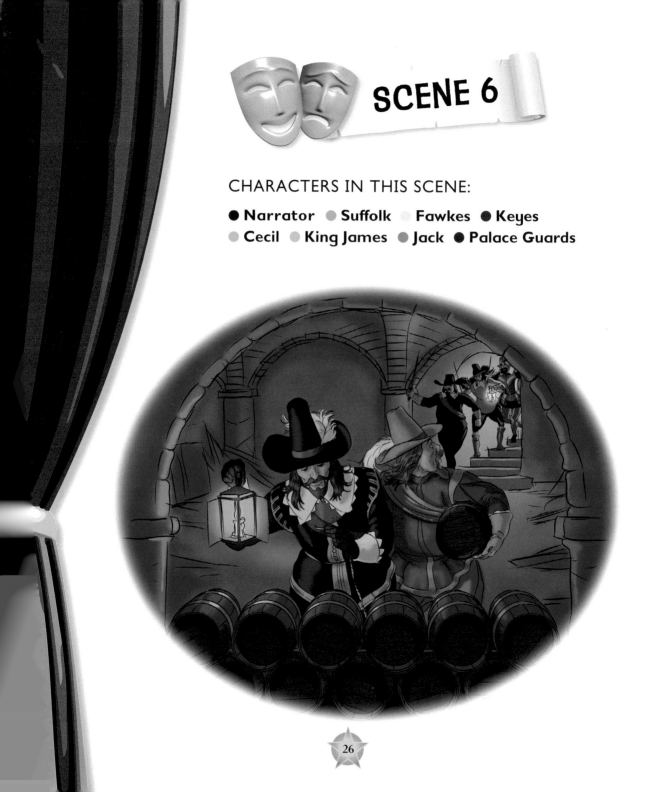

Guy Fawkes *and* **Robert Keyes** *are in the cellars surrounded by barrels of gunpowder.*

● **Narrator:** In the cellars under the Palace, Fawkes and Keyes are laying a trail of gunpowder from a giant stack of barrels to use as a fuse.

Fawkes: There, that should be enough. All clear, Keyes?

● **Keyes:** Are you sure this fuse is long enough, Fawkes? That amount of gunpowder will blow this place sky-high. Will we get out in time?

Fawkes: *(shrugging)* We should have a couple of minutes. *(grinning)* Right, got a match?

● **Keyes:** I want to light the fuse, Fawkes, please! I just love to light the fuse.

Fawkes: Oh, go on then! *(Hands the match to **Keyes**.)*

Keyes *grins and lights the fuse, which starts to hiss. Just then* **Cecil** *arrives with* **Jack**, **Monteagle**, **Suffolk** *and the* **Palace Guards**.

● **Cecil:** Stop, you villains! Seize them, Guards!

*The **guards** rush at **Fawkes** and **Keyes**, who draw their swords. There's a huge fight, with much yelling and cursing.*

Fawkes: Hah, you'll never take us alive! You're all going to die!

Jack: *(spotting the fire racing up the fuse towards the gunpowder)* Not if I can help it! *(He runs over and stamps out the fire just in time.)*

Cecil: *(looking at **Jack** proudly)* Well done, Jack! *(looking at **Fawkes** and **Keyes**)* Surrender, you men!

*The struggle goes on for a while, but **Fawkes** and **Keyes** are finally overcome. The **guards** disarm them, pushing them onto their knees.*

Cecil: I want the names of the other plotters.

Fawkes: Down with the king! You'll get no names from me.

Keyes: Nor from me. Mr Catesby wouldn't like us to tell you his name. Er... whoops! Oh, deary me...

Fawkes: *(furious)* You fool, Keyes!

Cecil: Ah, Robert Catesby. I know him well. We'll soon track him down and when we do, I'm sure he'll lead us to the others.

*The **guards** lead **Fawkes** and **Keyes** away.*

Jack: What will happen to them, Sir?

Cecil: Nothing very pleasant. They'll probably be **tortured** and then **executed**. After they've been put on trial, of course.

Suffolk: Quite right, too!

*Just then the **king** arrives with some more **Palace Guards**.*

King James: What's going on down here, Cecil? Who were those wretched men being taken away?

Cecil: No one you need worry about, Your Majesty.

King James: *(beckoning)* Well, come along. I'll be making my speech soon.

Cecil: *(rolling his eyes at **Jack**)* I wouldn't miss it for the world, Sire.

*They all leave the cellars, following the **king**.*

The End

GLOSSARY

Catholic
someone who believes the Pope is the head of their religion

execute
to carry out a death sentence

fuse
a length of material along which a flame moves to explode gunpowder

gunpowder
a type of explosive

Protestant
someone who believes that the king or queen is head of the Church of England

torture
to cause someone a lot of pain

First published in paperback in 2015

Copyright © Wayland 2015

Wayland
An imprint of
Hachette Children's Group
Part of Hodder & Stoughton
Carmelite House
50 Victoria Embankment
London EC4Y 0DZ

Editor: Katie Woolley
Designer: Elaine Wilkinson
Illustrator: Carlo Molinari

Dewey Number: 822.9'2-dc22
ISBN: 978 0 7502 9754 7

10 9 8 7 6 5 4 3 2 1

Printed in China

An Hachette UK company.
www.hachette.co.uk
www.hachettechildrens.co.uk

MIX
Paper from responsible sources
FSC® C104740
FSC
www.fsc.org